Puppies Have Paws
Kittens Have Claws

By Keith Lawrence Roman

Puppies Have Paws Kittens Have Claws

Morningside Books Softcover Edition

Published in the United States of America by

Morningside Books, Orlando, Florida

This edition is cataloged as:

ISBN 978-0-9827288-5-7

MorningsideBooks.net

Printed in the United States of America

Puppies Have Paws
Kittens Have Claws

Puppies have paws

Kittens have claws

Which would you rather be?

If you were a puppy you could bark loud

If you were a kitten you could meow

Which of these two is your favorite sound?

Kittens will scratch

and climb up on the couch

Puppies play catch outside of the house

Kittens chase mice

Puppies play nice

Which would you rather do
Play in the house or capture a mouse?

A kitten will climb to the top of a tree
Then cry out for help,

"Someone please rescue me"

A puppy will wander away from its home
Then whimper and whine,

"Oh, I'm so all alone"

Puppies and kittens both get into trouble

When there's one of each the trouble is double

There are puppies with spots

Some kittens wear socks

Some puppies are white

Some kittens are black

Some puppies and kittens even wear hats

Both puppies and kittens have soft fluffy fur

But puppies will yip and kittens will purr

Kittens have eyes that see in the dark

A puppy's sharp nose
leads it all through the park

They are so much alike but so far apart

Puppies have paws

Kittens have claws

The difference is easy to see

But if you could choose,
one of the two

Which then would you rather be?